# Burgoo Stew

A Richard Jackson Book

# BURGOO

Story by Susan Patron
Pictures by Mike Shenon

# STEW

Orchard Books / New York

For my parents, George and Rubye Hall — S.P.

Orchard Books, A division of Franklin Watts, Inc.
387 Park Avenue South, New York, NY 10016

Manufactured in the United States of America. Printed by General Offset Company, Inc. Bound by Horowitz/Rae. Book design by Mike Shenon. The text of this book is set in 16 pt. Caslon 540. The illustrations are ink line and watercolor drawings reproduced in full color.

10  9  8  7  6  5  4  3  2  1

Library of Congress Cataloging-in-Publication Data
Patron, Susan. Burgoo stew / story by Susan Patron ; pictures by Mike Shenon.  p.  cm.
"A Richard Jackson book." Summary: In this variant of "Stone Soup," old Billy Que tames a group of rough hungry boys.
ISBN 0-531-05916-2. — ISBN 0-531-08516-3 (lib.)
[1. Folklore—France.  2. Soups—Folklore.]  I. Shenon, Mike, ill.  II. Title.  PZ8.1.P2318Bu
1991  398.21′0944—dc20  [E]  90-43791

A crowd of five rowdy bad boys set out to the edge of town to find old Billy Que. They'd been so quarrelsome and contrary that even their own mamas had shooed them away. Their stomachs were empty and their eyes were flashing trouble!

They wanted to see if Billy Que had anything good to eat, and if he did, they aimed
to steal it.

They found him hunkered down outside by
his big old black cooking pot. Billy Que looked

at those bad boys with their big knuckly hands
and their bright, cantankerous eyes.

"You give us to eat!" they yelled, and,
cranky-mad, kicked the dirt with their big
feet.

"You give us all your food!" they shouted, and, feisty-mad, crowded in close to old Billy Que.

Billy Que wasn't afraid. He knew those boys
—had known them since they were wee hungry lads.

"I could make some Burgoo Stew, which is
the best thing of all when you're hungry," he
said. "And it's even good when you're not.
It's just about the best stew in the world because I always stir in a secret ingredient—
something you can't see or smell or touch or
taste."

"Give us Burgoo Stew; show us how to make it!" hollered those big mean hungry boys.

"You boys got to fill up the cooking pot with water and light the fire underneath," said Billy Que, "while I work on finding the secret ingredient."

So the five boys filled the big pot with water. They built a fire under the pot and lit it.

"Now will you kindly go up to the house and fetch the salt and pepper, and my basket of dried herbs—that's all I need to make delicious Burgoo Stew."

And as those boys turned away toward the house, they heard a loud PLOP in the stew-pot water.

"What was that?" they demanded.

"That was the stone what holds down the secret ingredient I just threw in," said Que. "Without that ingredient, this wouldn't be such a fine stew a-tall. Now go after that salt and pepper, and if any of you boys has a mama with an onion she don't need, you ask her kindly for it."

The first skinny, weedy big boy with holes in his shoes remembered his mama had a wicker basket full of onions, though not much of anything else. He ran home faster than water runs downhill.

"This Burgoo Stew is beginning to cook up just right, because the magic ingredient's started working," said Billy Que. "Now I wonder whose mama has a carrot she could spare?"

The second mean-looking big boy with snarls in his hair remembered his mama had a bunch of carrots, though not very much of anything else. "Ask her kindly," said Billy Que, and that boy ran home as fast as a strong wind blowing leaves.

"Ah, it's beginning to simmer as only Burgoo Stew simmers," said Que. "Doesn't look like much yet, but that magic ingredient's working even stronger. It's near perfect now, but what would make this stew the best ever is a plain turnip. Course, strictly speaking, we don't need it . . . but a turnip would be nice."

The third lanky, cranky big boy with dirt behind his ears remembered that his mama had a few turnips, though not very much of anything else. He ran home faster than a stone sinks in a pond. He had it in his mind that just once, just maybe, he'd ask his mama kindly.

Billy Que stirred that Burgoo Stew slowly and leaned over to smell it with his long, bony nose. "Ah," he said happily. "Now the magic ingredient is well mixed in. I have not made a stew this good in about thirty years! One thing, though, that I guess would be scrumptious—a little hunk of fresh meat; just some small stringy bony hunk is enough, if anyone's mama had some to spare."

The fourth scrawny, naughty big boy with smudges on his forehead remembered that his mama had some hunks of meat, though not very much of anything else. He thought that maybe, if he asked her kindly, she'd give him one. And he ran home faster than drops of rain fall to the ground.

"This stew doesn't need anything else to be finer than a summer day in the mountains," said Billy Que, stirring. "Although my own dear mama used to like to put in a potato sometimes. Yes, a wee potato sounds just about right for this particular stew."

The fifth rough-tough big boy with grease on his knuckles remembered that his mama had a sack of potatoes, though not very much

of anything else. "Kindly," he thought. "I'll ask her kindly." And he ran home faster than boys run when they're hungry.

Billy Que hunkered down by his big cooking pot and kept an eye on the fire. He smiled, because he did enjoy having company, especially when he was cooking Burgoo Stew.

The five boys came running back. They carried lumpy things in their pockets, in their

shirttails, and clutched in their mitts, and one
boy had a bulb of garlic in his cuff.

When Billy Que washed everything, he no-
ticed that the boys' mamas had kindly sent a
number of onions, several carrots and turnips,

a goodly hunk of meat, and more potatoes than
he could hold in his two hands. He put them
all in the pot and stirred slowly, and added

salt and pepper and herbs and the garlic, and
pretty soon the boys could smell that Burgoo
Stew, too.

"There are six wooden bowls up to the house, and six pewter spoons, and six blue napkins, and a big loaf of fresh-baked bread," said Que. "Would someone kindly fetch them?"

And four big boys with flashing eyes ran to
the house, while the fifth stood sniffing and
sniffing the stew.

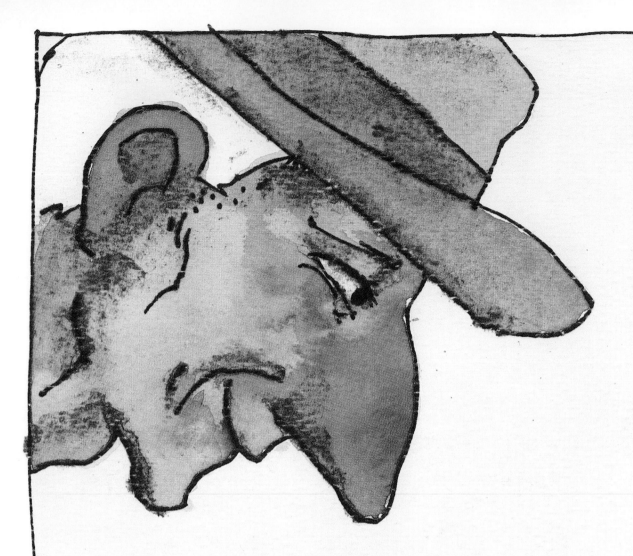

"Burgoo Stew! Made from practically nothing, plus a special magic secret ingredient! Allow me to serve you, my friends," said Billy Que, and he filled each bowl right up.

The five boys ate their stew and then

_kindly_

asked for more.

$\mathbf{A}$nd from that day on, they were still big and rough and knuckly and weedy and rowdy and dirty and lanky and cranky and scrawny and naughty, with snarls in their hair, but they were never, ever quite so bad or quite so hungry again.